THEY SAY
BLUE

JILLIAN TAMAKI

ⓖ

GROUNDWOOD BOOKS
HOUSE OF ANANSI PRESS
TORONTO   BERKELEY

They say blue is the
colour of the sky.

Which is true today!

They say the
sea is blue, too.

It certainly looks
like it from here.

But when I hold the
water in my hands, it's
as clear as glass.

I toss it up in the air to make diamonds.

What about a blue whale?
Is a blue whale blue?

I don't know.
I've never seen a blue
whale . . .

. . . but I don't need to crack an egg to know it holds an orange yolk inside.

I can't see my blood,
but I know it's red. It moves
around my body even when
I am perfectly still.

And when we play,
I feel it race faster
to keep up.

A field of grass looks
like a golden ocean.

If I built a boat that was
light enough, maybe
I could sail upon it.

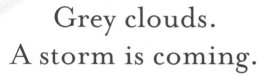

Grey clouds.
A storm is coming.

I could never build a boat
light enough to sail on a
golden ocean.

It's just plain old yellow
grass anyway.

They say spring means winter's over, but why does it still feel so cold?

Oh!
Could purple mean
something new?

It's warm at last.

I stretch to the sky
with my fingers
open wide.

I sprouted!

Standing tall, I angle my green
leaves to feel the sun.
I think I'll stay quiet and listen to
the sounds of the summer.

Fall arrives, and my leaves slowly turn brown. I drop them one by one and wiggle my toes in the soft pile at my feet.

Winter's come again.
Now the rest of the world
is quiet, too.

All white, up and down.
Sometimes I can't tell the
difference between the
land and sky.

I close my eyes.

Oh, I'm so sleepy . . .

Black is the colour
of my hair.

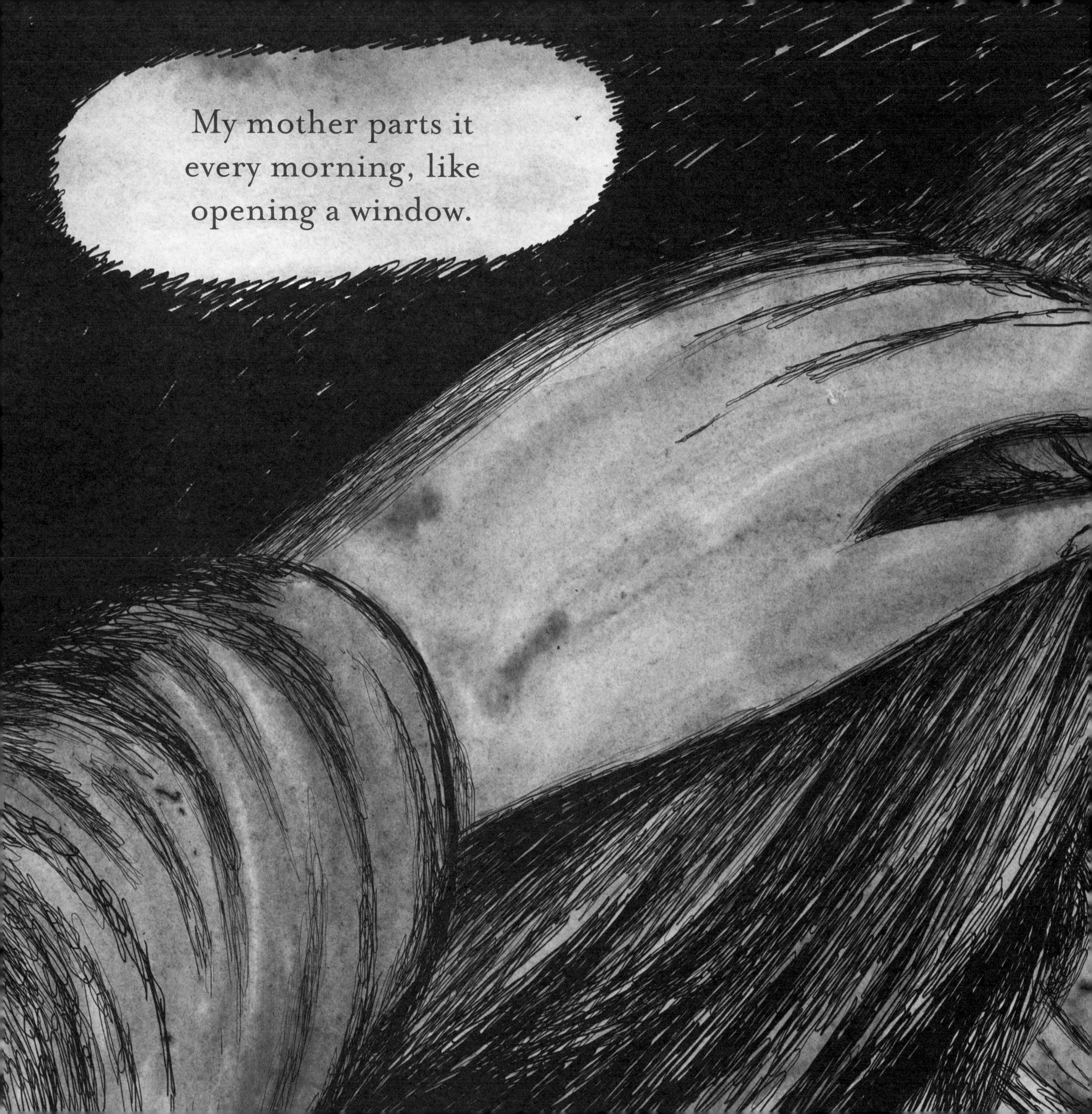
My mother parts it
every morning, like
opening a window.

Together we watch the black crows bob and chatter in the field outside.

We wonder what
they are thinking
when they look at us.
What they see.

Their dark eyes
won't tell.

They just pull their
big bodies into the air.

Tiny inkblots on
a sea of sky.

For my parents

Groundwood Books / House of Anansi Press
groundwoodbooks.com

We acknowledge for their financial support of our publishing
program the Canada Council for the Arts, the Ontario Arts
Council and the Government of Canada.

Canada Council   Conseil des Arts
for the Arts   du Canada

ONTARIO ARTS COUNCIL
CONSEIL DES ARTS DE L'ONTARIO
an Ontario government agency
un organisme du gouvernement de l'Ontario

With the participation of the Government of Canada | Canadä
Avec la participation du gouvernement du Canada

Library and Archives Canada Cataloguing in Publication
Tamaki, Jillian, author, illustrator
They say blue / [written and illustrated by] Jillian Tamaki.
Issued in print and electronic formats.
ISBN 978-1-77306-020-0 (hardcover). —
ISBN 978-1-77306-021-7 (PDF)
I. Title.
PS8639.A55T44 2018   jC813'.6   C2017-905254-3
C2017-905255-1

The illustrations were made with a combination of acrylic paint
on watercolour paper and Photoshop.
Design by Jillian Tamaki and Chad W. Beckerman
Printed and bound in Malaysia

FSC
www.fsc.org

MIX
Paper from
responsible sources
FSC® C012700